Hello, Family Members,

Learning to read is one of the most important accomplishments of early childhood. **Hello Reader!** books are designed to help children become skilled readers who like to read. Beginning readers learn to read by remembering frequently used words like "the," "is," and "and"; by using phonics skills to decode new words; and by interpreting picture and text clues. These books provide both the stories children enjoy and the structure they need to read fluently and independently. Here are suggestions for helping your child.

- Have your child think about a word he or she does not recognize right away. Provide hints such as "Let's see if we know the sounds" and "Have we read other words like this one?"
- Encourage your child to use phonics skills to sound out new words.
- Provide the word for your child when more assistance is needed so that he or she does not struggle and the experience of reading with you is a positive one.
- Encourage your child to have fun by reading with a lot of expression . . . like an actor!

I do hope that you and your child enjoy this book.

　　　　　—Francie Alexander
　　　　　Reading Specialist,
　　　　　Scholastic's Learning Ventures

D0187111

Activity Pages
In the back of the book are skill-building activities. These are designed to give children further reading and comprehension practice and to provide added enjoyment. Offer help with directions as needed and encourage your child to have FUN with each activity.

Game Cards
In the middle of the book are eight pairs of game cards. These are designed to help your child become more familiar with words in the book and to play fun games.

- Have your child use the word cards to find matching words in the story. Then have him or her use the picture cards to find matching words in the story.
- Play a matching game. Here's how: Place the cards face up. Have your child match words to pictures. Once the child feels confident matching words to pictures, put cards face down. Have the child lift one card, then lift a second card to see if both match. If the cards match, the child can keep them. If not, place the cards face down once again. Keep going until he or she finds all matches.

For Karen, with love.
—K. W.

ISBN 0-439-09908-0

Text copyright © 1999 by Kimberly Weinberger.
Illustrations copyright ©1999 by Diane deGroat.
All rights reserved. Published by Scholastic Inc.
SCHOLASTIC, HELLO READER, CARTWHEEL BOOKS and associated logos
are trademarks and/or registered trademarks of Scholastic Inc.

Library of Congress Cataloging-in-Publication Data available.

10 9 8 7 6 5 4 3 2 1   9/9 0/0 01 02 03 04

Printed in the U.S.A.   24
First printing, November1999

Our Thanksgiving

by Kimberly Weinberger
Illustrated by Diane deGroat

· ·

My First Hello Reader!
With Game Cards

· ·

SCHOLASTIC INC.

New York   Toronto   London   Auckland   Sydney
New Delhi   Mexico City   Hong Kong

Thanksgiving is a
busy day.

"Hurry! Guests are on their way."

"Are the sweet potatoes made?"

Time to watch the
big parade.

Now the family is here.

"How you've grown
in just one year!"

Turkey, stuffing . . .
where's my plate?

I lift my fork.
Mom says, "Wait!

potatoes

parade

turkey

plate

fork

stuffing

home

family

"Let's give thanks for all
we see . . .

"Our friends, our home,
and family.

"Let's give thanks for food
and fun."

Now Thanksgiving has begun!

A Thanksgiving Feast

Point to the things you might find at a
Thanksgiving dinner.
Now point to the things you would not find
at a Thanksgiving dinner.

Family

How do you think the children in this story
feel when they greet their Grandma?
How do you feel when relatives visit?
How do you think your relatives feel when
they see you?

What's Wrong?

Point to the five things that are wrong at this Thanksgiving dinner.

A Dot-to-Dot
Thanksgiving Surprise

Connect the dots from A to Z for a
Thanksgiving surprise.

Rhyme Time

Rhyming words sound alike. The words **day** and **way** are rhyming words.
Match each picture with the word that rhymes.

home

day

sweet

plate

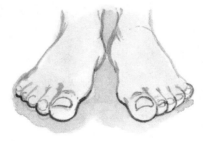

ANSWERS

A Thanksgiving Feast

You might find:

You would not find:

Family

Answers will vary.

What's Wrong?

These things are wrong:

A Dot-to-Dot
Thanksgiving Surprise

Rhyme Time

home

day

sweet

plate